Cinderella

by

Leonard Matthews

BROCKHAMPTON PRESS
LONDON

ELLA was a little girl living at home with her mother and father. They were all happy together until the day Ella's mother died.

Several years later, Ella's father remarried. His new wife had two daughters of her own and Ella's father hoped that the three girls would all be friends.

All went well until Ella's father, who went on long sea voyages, was reported missing after the ship he was sailing in was wrecked.

ELLA then found her life was very different. Her step-mother let her daughters do what they liked and one thing they liked as they grew up, was that Ella should do all the housework.

The sisters were unkind to Ella in many little ways, like whispering and laughing at her behind her back. They passed her their clothes to mend and when they wore out they gave them to her. She was made to cook and serve the meals and told to stay in the kitchen.

IN the winter evenings, because her clothes were worn, Ella was pleased to be in the kitchen near the big fire. There, she and a friendly mouse could keep warm. That was why Ella came to be known as Cinderella.

Although Cinderella's life had changed, she was still kind when people or animals needed help. As she grew older she became more beautiful and the more beautiful Cinderella became, the less pleasant were her jealous step-sisters.

SHE had been sent out to do the family shopping one afternoon when she read a sign about a dance on the village green.

Cinderella's heavy shopping basket was forgotten in the excitement of thinking of the dance later that day. She did hope that she would be able to go. Cinderella loved to dance.

IT was a happy Cinderella who prepared tea for her step-mother and step-sisters and as soon as they had finished and the washing-up was done, Cinderella went to the kitchen cupboard.

From the cupboard she took a dress and coat. They were her best clothes and she had made them from old clothes given her by her step-sisters.

She changed quickly and after saying goodbye to her friendly mouse, she quietly closed the door and hurried towards the village green.

WHILE Cinderella was on her way to the dance, the Crown Prince who was out with one of his huntsmen, read a notice about it. He decided to go along.

The prince did not want to be recognised, so he and his huntsman exchanged clothes. They even changed wigs!

It was as she reached the village green, Cinderella found that the young man walking beside her, was also going to the dance.

"WILL you have the first dance with me?" asked the young man. "I don't know many young ladies in this village."

"Of course," Cinderella, smiled, knowing how it felt to be alone. She knew all the young men in the village and although they would have liked to dance with her, they had no opportunity. The prince and Cinderella were getting on so well together.

AS the dance ended, the young man told Cinderella who he was and gave her an invitation to the ball his father was giving the next week.

Cinderella was happy.

As the week went by Cinderella's happy dreams disappeared. How could she go to the ball? She had no ball gown or pretty shoes.

On the evening of the ball, when she had finished all her work she sat warming herself by the fire, and telling her friend the mouse about the ball she was missing.

SHE, heard her step-mother and step-sisters leave for the ball. Then suddenly there was a flash of light and standing in front of her appeared a beautiful lady.

"I am your fairy godmother," she told Cinderella, "and I'm going to help you get ready to go to the ball."

Cinderella was amazed. She had never known she had a fairy godmother.

"But I have no ball gown," said Cinderella.

"COME into the garden with me," smiled the Fairy Godmother, "and please bring the pumpkin with you."

Then she asked Cinderella to call four of her little mice friends. The Fairy Godmother spoke to them and they went and stood in front of the pumpkin.

Cinderella did not understand what was happening.

THE next moment, her Fairy Godmother waved her magic wand amid a flurry of tiny stars!

Cinderella found that she was dressed in a beautiful ball gown. The pumpkin had become a splendid coach and the four mice had changed into four fine white horses. Cinderella was speechless.

Her Godmother smiled at her gently. "Enjoy yourself," she said, as she disappeared, "but be sure to be home by midnight or your ball gown will vanish and you will be poor Cinderella again."

WHEN the coach arrived at the palace, Cinderella saw the prince welcoming his guests.

The very moment he saw Cinderella step from the coach he came to greet her. "Thank you for accepting my invitation," he said. "Let us go into the palace and join the other guests."

CINDERELLA was thrilled to be taken into the ballroom by the prince and as soon as they arrived, the orchestra began to play. The prince led Cinderella on to the dance floor and they danced together the whole evening, just as they had on the village green. There was a difference though. This time they fell in love.

TIME slipped by for Cinderella and she forgot her godmother's warning that she must leave the ball before midnight.

It was not until the midnight chimes were ringing that she remembered. She listened carefully and counted them.

HOW she wished she had left the ball earlier.

She wept as her beautiful ball gown changed back into her ragged dress.

The prince was shocked and unable to speak.

CINDERELLA just turned and ran as fast as she could and as she ran, one of the pretty shoes fell from her foot.

The prince picked it up and called to Cinderella but she took no notice even if she heard him. All she wanted to do was get back home as fast as she could.

IMMEDIATELY, the prince sent for his Prime Minister. He gave him Cinderella's slipper and told him to sit down.

"You must find the beautiful girl who owns this slipper," he said. "The ball was held for me to find a wife and I found her this evening. I wish to marry the girl who was wearing this slipper."

THE Prime Minister sent out a proclamation that the prince would marry the girl whose foot fitted the glass slipper.

After looking for many weeks for Cinderella, the Prime Minister went on a house to house search for her. At last he came to the house where Cinderella lived.

Her two step-sisters could hardly wait to try on the slipper. They were so sure it would fit one of them. How disappointed they were. The slipper was too small for both of them.

"ARE there any other young ladies living here?" asked the Prime Minister.

"Well, there's Cinderella," said one of the sisters. "But she doesn't count," said the other.

"Oh yes, she does," said the Prime Minister and when Cinderella tried on the slipper, it fitted her foot perfectly.

"Hooray!" said the Prime Minister and dashed off to fetch the prince.

THE prince hurried to Cinderella's home. How delighted he was to see that the girl whose foot had fitted the slipper, was the girl he loved.

"Shall we be married at once?" he asked Cinderella.

They were, of course, and lived happily ever after.